THE DANGEROUS
LIVES OF THE
JACOBITES

D1638990

For Seren, Ben, Ruaridh, Poppy, Abigail, Elissa
and all Scotland's children – L.S.

To Eleni, who believed and supported me every day
to help make my dreams come true – D.G.

Kelpies is an imprint of Floris Books
First published in 2019 by Floris Books

The publisher acknowledges subsidy from Creative Scotland
towards the publication of this volume

 Also available as an eBook

British Library CIP data available
ISBN 978-178250-596-9
Printed & bound by MBM Print SCS Ltd, Glasgow

 Floris Books supports sustainable forest management
by printing this book on materials made from wood that
comes from responsible sources and reclaimed material

MIX
Paper from
responsible sources
FSC® C117931

FACT-TASTIC STORIES FROM SCOTLAND'S HISTORY

THE DANGEROUS LIVES OF THE JACOBITES

WRITTEN BY LINDA STRACHAN

ILLUSTRATED BY DARREN GATE

Young Kelpies

CONTENTS

WHO WERE THE JACOBITES?

The Jacobites were supporters of the Stuart royal family, who had ruled Scotland for over 300 years, and England and Ireland since 1603. Many of the Stuart kings were called James, and the name Jacobite comes from the Latin *Jacobus* = James. There were four main Jacobite Risings in 1689, 1715, 1719 and 1745 when the Jacobites fought against the government because...

Ernest Augustus of Hanover ── Sophia of Hanover

William II of Orange (Dutch Republic) ── Mary

The House of Hanover

LINE OF SUCCESSION

George I
ruled 1714-1727 ── Sophia Dorothea

William III (of Orange)
ruled 1689-1702

5 George of Hanover, a great-grandson of James VI, came from Germany to become king instead. The Jacobites were not happy.

George II
ruled 1727-1760 ── Caroline

2 King James VII fled to France when his Protestant daughter Mary came from the Dutch Republic with her husband William to become king and queen. Many people believed James VII should still be king. They called themselves the Jacobites.

Army commander 1745

William Augustus, Duke of Cumberland

7 other children

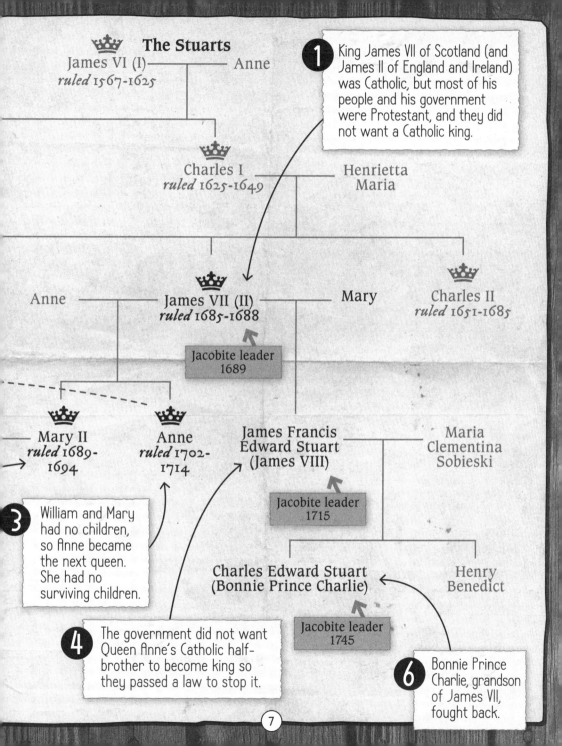

The Stuarts

James VI (I)
ruled 1567-1625 — Anne

1 King James VII of Scotland (and James II of England and Ireland) was Catholic, but most of his people and his government were Protestant, and they did not want a Catholic king.

Charles I
ruled 1625-1649 — Henrietta Maria

Anne — James VII (II)
ruled 1685-1688 — Mary — Charles II *ruled 1651-1685*

Jacobite leader 1689

Mary II
ruled 1689-1694

Anne
ruled 1702-1714

James Francis Edward Stuart (James VIII) — Maria Clementina Sobieski

Jacobite leader 1715

3 William and Mary had no children, so Anne became the next queen. She had no surviving children.

Charles Edward Stuart (Bonnie Prince Charlie) — Henry Benedict

Jacobite leader 1745

4 The government did not want Queen Anne's Catholic half-brother to become king so they passed a law to stop it.

6 Bonnie Prince Charlie, grandson of James VII, fought back.

1. BONNIE PRINCE CHARLIE AND THE JACOBITE CAUSE

ROB MACDONALD, AGE 14, SUMMER 1745

I joined the Jacobite army on a midsummer's day in the year of our Lord 1745. My sister Aggie was coming home carrying a basket of nettles, and Granny was knitting in the sunshine outside the croft.

I had been out to check on the cattle. I could smell bannocks cooking before I stepped inside, and it made my stomach rumble. I tried to sneak around Mother to grab one off the hot girdle iron, but she rapped me on the knuckles with her wooden spoon.

"Leave them be, Rob, you'll get yours when they're ready."

"Will Father be back soon?" I asked. He'd been away for a few days now.

"Soon, Rob. He's just gone to settle something with the clan chief," Mother told me, as Aggie stepped inside. "Ah, there ye are, Aggie. Bring those nettles here for the soup, then away and call Meggie in."

"Race you to the midden and back, Aggie!" I ran out and around the back of the croft, while Aggie grabbed up her skirts and chased after me. We ran past our younger sister Meggie,

who was carefully carrying a basket of eggs. She put it down and tried to catch us, but she tripped over and started bawling. I stopped and picked her up, twirling her around to make her giggle.

"I beat you, Rob!" Aggie shouted from the doorway.

"Not fair, Aggie!" I grinned.

FACT-TASTIC FACT

DON'T FALL IN THE MIDDEN!

The midden was a compost heap for all household waste, including bones and shells. In Scotland people say "You're a midden!" to mean you're messy or scruffy.

We were just about to have our soup and warm bannocks when Father arrived home with a wide smile on his face.

"He has come!" Father shouted. "Prince Charlie has landed on the Western Isles, and we're to meet him at Glenfinnan."

He picked up wee Meggie and Aggie, one in each arm, and swung them around until they were dizzy. I roared with joy and threw my bonnet in the air. We'd been hearing about

Prince Charlie and the Jacobite Cause since we were old enough to listen.

My heart thundered with pride when Father announced that he and I were going to join Prince Charlie's army, and gather more men on the way. Mother looked worried, but proud too.

"Why can't I go?" asked Aggie. "I'm as fast as Rob."

"No," Mother said firmly. "I will need you here, to help me with the animals and all the other things Rob and your father would normally do."

"It's an important job, lass," said Father.

But Aggie stomped off in a huff.

The next day, Father and I set off together. I had no idea how long it would be before I saw my family again. We walked fast over soggy bogland, heading west up craggy hills and across rushing rivers. I thought I'd be able to keep up with Father, but by the third day I was fair done in and I sank down on a cairn.

"I'm bone weary, Father. Can we no stop for a bit?"

He turned, leaning on his long staff. "I know I'm pushing ye, lad, but we canna let the Prince down."

We stopped off at other townships like ours to pass on the news. Father was mostly welcomed like an old friend. He was a tacksman and everyone knew and respected him. But I was surprised that some of the clansmen didn't want to join the Prince's army.

I sat in the great hall of one of the big clan houses, where the men had gathered. Father stood by the huge fireplace talking to an elderly member of the clan, who said, "The Prince should never have come. He should go back to France and stay there."

"You are wrong. His father is our rightful king." Father said, in a quiet but strong voice. "You'll soon change your mind when the other clans come out to support the Prince."

"I see no reason to risk our lives for an Italian Prince," said the old man.

I could tell Father was angry – I was, too – but he didn't show it. He just shook his head.

BONNIE PRINCE CHARLIE
(1720–1788)

BONNIE PRINCE CHARLIE

- Prince Charles was the grandson of **King James VII (II of England and Wales)**.

- He grew up in Rome in a palace owned by the Pope.

- His full name was **Charles Edward Louis Philip Casimir Maria Stuart**. His father called him **Carluccio**. Many people at the time called him the **Young Pretender**. He has become known as **Bonnie Prince Charlie**.

- He was only 24 years old when he fought against the British government to make his father **James Francis Edward Stuart** (known as the **Old Pretender**), king.

- In the summer of 1745 he set sail for Britain with **French soldiers and weapons**. After a fierce battle with the British Royal Navy off the coast of Cornwall, his battleship, the *Elizabeth*, carrying his army and weapons, was forced to return to France. But Prince Charles was determined to keep fighting.

- His boat, the *Du Teillay*, landed on the Western Isles of Scotland on 23rd July 1745, and headed for the mainland. The **Jacobite Rising of '45** had begun.

BATTLE AT SEA

The *Elizabeth*

This **French man-of-war ship** carried Prince Charlie's army and weapons. The British, French and Spanish naval fleets used this type of battleship.

The *Du Teillay*

Prince Charlie sailed alongside his army on this smaller **frigate**. After the battle he carried on towards Scotland.

Carried 700 men

64 guns

Weighed 1,000 tons

Carried 67 men

16–18 guns

Faster than bigger warships

Broadsides

The HMS *Lion*

This **British Royal Navy man-of-war ship** was very like the *Elizabeth*. Its crew was determined to stop Prince Charlie arriving in Britain.

The HMS *Lion* and the *Elizabeth* fired at each other from their **broadsides** in a tactic called **'line of battle'**. The biggest ship with the most powerful weapons usually won. In this battle, both ships were badly damaged, many men were injured and killed, and both ships had to retreat.

HIGHLAND CLANS

The Highlanders spoke **Scots Gaelic**. Only the children of land owners learned English, and sometimes French and Italian.

In Gaelic *clann* means children.

The **clan chief** lived in a large house or castle and owned the land. He obeyed government laws but also made laws for his people. His **clanspeople** often lived in small groups of crofts called townships, and were fiercely loyal to their chief.

Most people were very poor. In the **countryside** they farmed oats, barley, kale and cattle.

In the bigger **towns** like Aberdeen, they worked in paper, woollens, cotton, linen and jute factories.

Highland **women** were well respected, unlike many women at the time who were expected to obey their husbands.

Highland men wore **plaids** – big tartan woollen blankets, folded and held on by belts. Plaids were the original kilts.

WORDS ARE IMPORTANT

The British government called the conflicts Rebellions, against King William and later King George. The Jacobites called them Risings – they were rising up to fight for their rightful king.

LOBSTERBACKS

The government soldiers were known as Redcoats because they wore long red jackets. Sometimes the Jacobites called them Lobsterbacks.

FACT-TASTIC FACT

When we finally reached the meeting point at Glenfinnan, the sun beat hot on our heads as we waited for the other clans to arrive. We stood at the top of the loch for a long time, and I secretly wondered if the old clansman had been right. Would no one else come to join the Prince's army?

Suddenly there was a cheer as the Camerons and the Keppoch MacDonalds arrived, bringing prisoners with them, including a captured Redcoat captain.

"What took you so long?" I asked one of them.

"Well, lad, we met some sixty or more government troops at High Bridge. There were just a dozen of us, but we got the better of them!" He laughed.

"What did you do?" I was amazed. How could twelve men beat sixty?

"We waited behind the inn, watching for them coming over the bridge. Wee Donald played his pipes while we ran in and out of the trees, yelling and waving our plaids, holding them wide. They thought we were an army and were so feart that they wouldn't cross the bridge at all. Their commander sent his servant and the captain across, so we took them prisoner, and the rest ran away!"

Just then we heard more cheering and I scrambled up onto a rock. There were hundreds of folk gathered all around us. I'd never seen so many people in one place before! I looked towards the loch and caught my first glimpse of Prince Charlie. There he was, in a blue jacket, holding his sword high.

"I can see him!" I yelled down to my father.

I could hardly believe it – that I was there to welcome Prince Charlie home to Scotland. It was a rare sight, something I would remember all my days.

Father climbed up beside me and we watched the Prince's men lift his royal standard to announce the start of the Rising. My heart throbbed to the beat of the drum and the sound of all the clansmen, women and children cheering, me loudest of all.

But little did we know what that year would bring and how it would change our lives.

WERE THE JACOBITES ALL SCOTTISH?

No! The Jacobites were fighting to reclaim the thrones of Scotland, England and Ireland. Scottish Highlanders formed a large part of the Jacobite armies, but many Scots fought for the government side too. A mix of Scottish Highlanders and Lowlanders, and some English, Irish, Welsh and French soldiers made up the Jacobite army.

FACT-TASTIC FACT

AGGIE

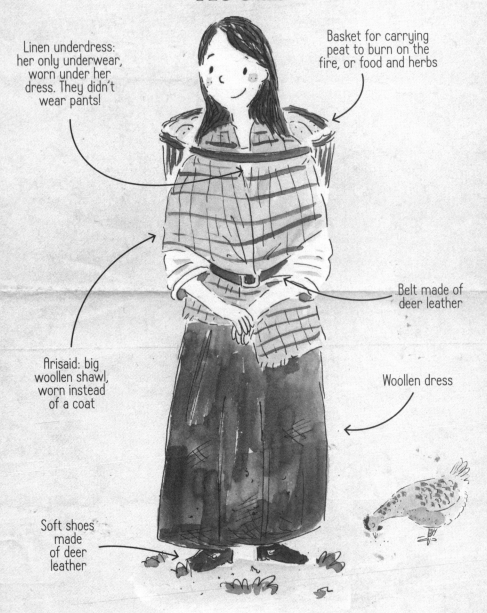

Linen underdress: her only underwear, worn under her dress. They didn't wear pants!

Basket for carrying peat to burn on the fire, or food and herbs

Arisaid: big woollen shawl, worn instead of a coat

Belt made of deer leather

Woollen dress

Soft shoes made of deer leather

2. THE TALE OF THE '89 RISING

AGGIE MACDONALD, AGE 12, SUMMER 1745

Father, Rob and most of the men in our township have been away for a few weeks now. It's worrying that there's no news of them. Mother, Meggie and I have been staying at the sheiling, up in the hills, with the other women. It feels a bit like a holiday, even though we have lots of work to do, making butter and cheese and looking after the animals. I miss Granny, though: she was not strong enough to climb into the hills, so she stayed behind.

Granny has taught me many ways to use the herbs, flowers and berries we grow or find in the wild.

Yesterday I made our neighbour Jeannie a drink to soothe her aching belly. When Rob cut his hand last spring chopping wood, I made a paste to stop the bleeding. Mother says it's a good thing to know because I can help our animals too, and without them we would starve.

What's a sheiling, Hen?

It's a little hut high up on the mountain pastures, where Highlanders took their cattle in summer.

Did the people sleep up there overnight?

Yes, it was a long, steep way to walk up and down every day.

Lovely views though, I bet, Hen.

That night sitting by the fire, I asked Mother to tell me more about the Jacobites.

"When I was a lass, not much older than you are," she said, "I remember Granny telling me the story of the very first Rising."

"Was Prince Charlie there?" I asked. "I thought he was much younger than you."

Mother smiled as she took out her knitting and nodded. "You're right, Aggie, our Prince Charlie is a young man. The first Rising was a long time ago, at the time of his grandfather, King James VII. That was until his daughter Mary and her husband William of Orange came from Europe and became king and queen. But many people in Scotland wanted James to be king again."

"Didn't they like the orange king?" asked Meggie.

"He wasn't orange!" Mother chuckled. "He was from a place called Orange in the Dutch Republic."

"But there was a battle, wasn't there?"

"Yes, Aggie, the Battle of Killiecrankie. I've never been there – it's far away from here – but this is what I was told. It's where the Highlands begin, a deep gorge with thick woods, and the River Garry runs down below. It was early evening in the middle of summer when the Jacobite army, led by Viscount Dundee, made their way up into the hills, out of sight of the government army. The government men, led by General Mackay, marched along the narrow pass down below, in the muddy glen."

"Did the Jacobites take the government army by surprise?"

"Well, Viscount Dundee waited until the sun had almost set, then the Highlanders ran down the hill towards their enemy. They fired their muskets and pistols then threw them down, because they didn't have time to reload them. Tossing off their plaids, they raised their swords and targes,

and charged down the hill yelling loudly."

I shivered. "That sounds scary."

"The government soldiers were terrified. Each time they fired their muskets, they had to stop to reload them again, by which point Dundee's men had reached them with their swords out and ready. Mackay's men ran away rather than fight the Highlanders."

"So, was that it finished?"

"Sadly, no, not quite. Mackay still had a whole regiment of cavalry waiting to fight. The Jacobites went on to win, but Viscount Dundee was killed."

"Oh no, that's horrible."

Mother hugged me close. "Battles are never easy. Many brave men were killed on both sides."

"But if the Jacobites won, how did the Rising fail?"

"They won that battle, Aggie, but there were more. The Jacobites had lost their great general, Dundee, and their new commander was not as clever. They fought and lost at Dunkeld, where the government troops hid in the houses and winding streets, and took the Jacobites by surprise. Then they lost at the Battle of Cromdale, and it was all over until the next time."

"How many Risings were there, Mother?"

"There have been four others, before now." Mother sighed. "Sadly none of them succeeded."

I grinned at her. "Don't you worry, this one will. Father said so!"

BOOM!

Grenades were first used in Britain at the Battle of Killiecrankie. They looked a bit like a cartoon bomb.

BATTLE REPORT: *Killiecrankie*

When: 27th July 1689

Size of armies:
Jacobites 2500
Government 5000

Weapons:
Jacobites: muskets, broadswords and targes.

Government: cannons, muskets and bayonets.

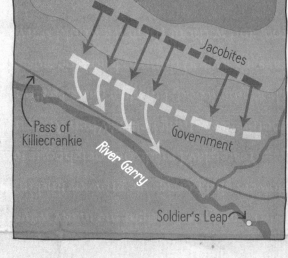

Tactics: The Jacobites watched from above the Pass of Killiecrankie then ran downhill in a terrifying Highland charge. The government soldiers didn't have time to reload their muskets or attach their bayonets.

Casualties: Jacobites 1,000, Government 1,200.

Outcome: The Jacobites won in just 30 minutes, but Viscount Dundee died.

SOLDIER'S LEAP

During the Battle of Killiecrankie, one government soldier, Donald McBean, escaped by leaping 5 ½ metres over the fast-flowing River Garry.

FACT-TASTIC FACT

VISCOUNT DUNDEE
(1648–1689)

- Viscount Dundee's name was **Laird John Graham Claverhouse.** He was known by his enemies as **Bluidy Clavers** and by Jacobites as **Bonnie Dundee.**

- He was King James VII's general in Scotland.

- In March 1689 when William III and Mary were declared king and queen instead of James VII, Viscount Dundee stormed out of the Scottish parliament. He lifted King James VII's royal standard and started the **'89 Rising.** He gathered an army of Highlanders to fight against

VISCOUNT DUNDEE

the new government. Most of his army had not fought in battle before but he trained them well.

WHAT HAPPENED NEXT?

1690
King William III defeated James VII at the **Battle of the Boyne** in Ireland.

1691
King William offered peace to all clan chiefs who swore an **Oath of Allegiance** to him.

1692
The Massacre of Glencoe
The chief of the MacDonalds of Glencoe signed the Oath of Allegiance a few days late, so a government official ordered that his entire clan be killed: "cut off root and branch." A regiment of soldiers from clan Campbell were staying with their old enemies, the MacDonalds, due to bad weather, under the Highland Code of Hospitality. They were told their gruesome orders and murdered 38 of the MacDonalds as they slept.

1694
Queen Mary II died, King William III's wife.

1701
The Act of Settlement
The English government ruled that if King William or Anne, Mary's sister, should die without an heir, the crown would pass to their distant German Protestant cousins, NOT their Catholic half-brother James Francis Edward Stuart.

1701
King James VII died in exile.

1702
King William III died when his horse tripped over a mole hill.

The Jacobites used to secretly thank the mole by saying a toast "to the small gentleman in the black velvet jacket." **Anne became queen.**

QUEEN ANNE

1707
The Act of Union

The Act of Union joined the parliaments of England and Scotland as the United Kingdom of Great Britain.

Many Scots were unhappy about the union, although some clan chiefs were bribed to vote for it.

"We're bought and sold for English gold – such a parcel of rogues in a nation."
ROBERT BURNS

1708
The Rising That Never Was

King James VII's son (and Prince Charlie's father), **James Francis Edward Stuart,** set sail from France with an army of about 5,000 French and Irish soldiers, 5 man-of-war ships and 30 smaller boats. Which of these ruined the Rising?

1. James caught the measles.

2. His ships were damaged in storms.

3. The British Royal Navy chased the Jacobites all the way back to France.

Answer: All of them!

1714
Queen Anne died and George, her distant cousin from Germany, became king of Great Britain and Ireland.

1715
The Jacobites were not amused...

ROB

White cockade — the Jacobite symbol

Bonnet

Neck tie for protection from sword blades

Waistcoat

Woollen jacket

Targe

Long linen undershirt — their only underwear. They did not wear pants!

Belt made of deer leather to hold plaid in place

Sword

Dirk — carried by all clansmen

Simple leather sporran, holding supplies such as oatmeal

Tartan plaid — one big piece of cloth, carefully folded and secured at the waist with a belt

Woollen socks

Soft shoes made of deer leather

3. TALES OF THE '15 AND '19 RISINGS

ROB, SUMMER 1745

We'd been on the road for a few weeks, heading south through the Highlands towards Edinburgh. There were now more than 4,000 Jacobites in our army. While we walked, the older clansmen showed us how to hold our weapons in a fight, and how to keep our feet dry. I made friends with Jamie, another young lad. We stuck together and were soon good friends.

One night, Jamie poked me in the ribs. He was smiling. "Rob, did ye see that?"

"What?" I spun around looking for some rare sight, but I saw nothing but bundles of soldiers wrapped in their plaids.

"The Prince, Rob," Jamie whispered and he pointed across the hillside to where the Prince slept on the heather, like the rest of us, covered only with his plaid. "No airs and graces. He would be a man to look up to – if I wasn't so tall!" He grinned.

I rocked with laughter. Jamie was so tall almost everyone had to look up to speak to him.

KING JAMES VIII?

Prince Charlie's father, James Francis Edward Stuart, never became king, but his loyal Jacobite followers still called him King James and treated him like a king. He lived his whole life in exile, mostly in a palace in Rome that was owned by the Pope.

JAMES EDWARD STUART

KING GEORGE I

King George I was a German nobleman from the House of Hanover. He was not popular in Britain, but he was a Protestant, like most of the British people. During his 13-year reign, he did not learn English.

KING GEORGE I

One evening, when the sun was just lighting up the rooftops, we entered Perth. The crowds were cheering and the church bells were ringing as we followed our Prince, finely dressed in green and gold, riding a white horse. I felt like cheering too.

The Prince stayed in the town while we camped outside it. Around the campfires at night we learned a lot about the earlier Risings, although not everyone agreed on what had gone wrong.

"It was the Oath of Allegiance," said Jock, a short man with a deep voice and arms as thick as tree trunks. "If the clan chiefs had no signed that…"

"You're talkin rot, Jock," his brother Davy roared, making the men turn around and stare. "They'd nae choice. It was when German Geordie came on the throne. But then Mar won at Sheriffmuir…"

"He didnae really win," Jock interrupted, with a growl.

I jumped in quickly, hoping to stop them arguing. "Can you tell us what happened at Sheriffmuir, Jock?"

"Well, lads," Jock began, whittling a piece of wood as he spoke. "I do know a bit about that, if ye care to hear it."

Jamie nodded, as keen as I was. We drew closer to hear better above the noise of the campsite.

"It was the 'Fifteen', in 1715, when the Jacobites tried again. King James made the Earl of Mar commander of the Jacobites, and he started the Rising. After just one month his army controlled most of Scotland, except Stirling."

He looked up to make sure we were listening. "With an army of aboot 7,000 men he headed south to meet the enemy near Stirling, at Sheriffmuir."

I pointed at the campfires glittering around us. "Was the army as big as this one?"

"Aye, lad, if not bigger. They met the much smaller government army, which was led by the Duke of Argyll. Some say they won..."

"Of course they did!" his brother growled at him.

"Nae, Davy. It wasnae so simple. Mar should have finished the battle, but he went away instead and the enemy claimed it as their victory. By the time King James arrived, things were no going well for the Jacobites and he had tae go back to France."

I shivered despite the warmth of the fire.

BONUS BATTLE REPORT: *Preston*

Many people in England were also unhappy that George I was king. On the same day as the Battle of Sheriffmuir, a second army of Jacobites was fighting a government army in Preston in northern England.

Size of armies: Jacobites 2,500, Government 2,500

Outcome: The government army laid siege to the town, with the Jacobites inside. It is said that the inexperienced Jacobite leader hid in bed during the battle, before surrendering. The government army won and many Jacobites were captured or killed.

BATTLE REPORT: *Sheriffmuir*

When: 13th November 1715

Size of armies: Jacobites 7,000, Government 3,000

Terrain: On a freezing day on boggy moorland, the two armies struggled to find each other!

Casualties: Jacobites 250, Government 700

Outcome: There was no clear winner and both armies retreated at dusk. The government army returned to fight the next day, but the Jacobite army didn't turn up, so you could say the government won!

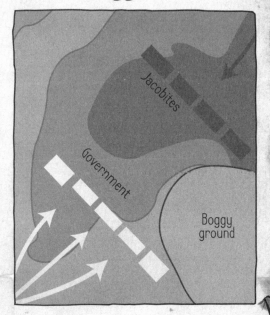

"But it wasn't long before the Jacobites tried again, was it?" I asked. I was sure I'd heard that from Father.

Jock continued. "The next Rising was just a few years later, 'the Nineteen' in 1719. You see, it was no just the Jacobites who wanted to put the Stuarts back on the throne: the Spanish were Catholics and they wanted it too."

"Go on," Jamie urged him. "What happened?"

Jock took a deep breath and carried on:

"Spanish soldiers were gathering in the Highlands at Eilean Donan castle to help the Jacobites."

"But there was a terrible storm, and the Spanish fleet with 5,000 men was wrecked at sea. Many clans thought the Rising was doomed and refused to join."

"With 1,000 men the Jacobites marched towards Inverness to fight the government troops, leaving some weapons behind in the castle."

"While they were gone, government ships sailed up to the castle, took the weapons and blew up all the gunpowder, destroying most of the castle."

"What happened next?" I asked, eager to hear the rest. Jock took his time, and sighed.

"The Jacobites fought the government at the Battle of Glen Shiel. But the government army had mortars and the Highlanders had no defence against them. Rob Roy MacGregor was one of the commanders at Glen Shiel."

"I'm a MacGregor, I've heard stories of Rob Roy," said Jamie.

"Aye, lad, he's well known," Jock replied. "He fought well, but sadly it was not enough. It was the end of the '19 Rising."

"We'll do better this time, won't we?" I asked, willing it to be true.

"That we will, lad." Davy grinned at me, and I truly believed him. I think we all did.

MORTAL MORTARS

Coehorn mortars were first used at the Battle of Glen Shiel. They were much smaller than cannons and could be moved by just 4 men. They fired deadly explosive shells.

ROB ROY MACGREGOR
(1671–1734)

Rob Roy fought for the Jacobites in the Battle of Sheriffmuir and survived the Battle of Glen Shiel. He was a well-known cattle drover and cattle thief. He borrowed money from noblemen, which he couldn't pay back, and had to go on the run. He was caught several times but always managed to escape. He lived to 63, which was old back then. Several books and films have been made about his life.

ROB ROY MACGREGOR

GENERAL WADE'S ROADS

In the 1720s and 30s General Wade, commander of the government forces in northern Britain, built 240 miles of roads, 40 bridges, and army barracks across Scotland, to make it easier to stop another rebellion. But he helped Jacobites to travel and communicate too.

If you had seen these roads before they were made you would lift up your hands and bless General Wade.

JACOBITE RHYME

WHAT HAPPENED NEXT?

1719

After the failed '19 Rising, **James Francis Edward Stuart** (aged 31) **married** Maria Clementina Sobieska, a Polish princess (aged only 16) – this was normal back then!

1720

Prince Charlie was born.

1720

George I died and **George II became King** of Great Britain and Ireland.

KING GEORGE II

1740–48

From 1740–48 most European countries were fighting each other in the **War of the Austrian Succession.** Britain, Austria, Germany and the Dutch Republic were fighting against France and several others. Most of the British navy and army were involved.

1743

Prince Charlie was named Prince Regent. His father made him **leader of the Jacobite Cause** following his own failed attempts.

1745

Prince Charlie had enough support from France to set sail for Britain...

4. 1745, EDINBURGH AND PRESTONPANS

ROB, SEPTEMBER 1745

During our days in Perth, the Prince himself taught us how to march and use our weapons.

"We're real soldiers now!" Jamie said proudly as we started our march south towards Edinburgh. We were at the front, alongside Father.

Dawn was breaking on a cold, bright morning when we arrived at the town of Edinburgh. I heard tell we had over 5,000 men now.

A SMELLY CITY

After 10 o'clock at night, when they heard the city drum beating, the people of Edinburgh emptied their chamber pots out of their windows. People in the streets had to watch out!

"Do you think they'll open the gates to us?" I asked Jamie. "What will we do if they don't?"

Jamie shrugged. "Maybe we'll have to lay siege to the town."

But we found the town gates open, which meant we definitely had friends in Edinburgh. It was a great day, the 17th September. It was my fifteenth birthday too, but there was no time to think about that.

We marched into the town following the Prince, who was in full Highland dress. The people of Edinburgh came out to see us pass by, and leaned out of windows above, cheering wildly. I felt ten feet tall as I waved back at them. An old lady handed Jamie and me a delicious warm bannock to share.

I'd never seen anywhere like Edinburgh, with its tall buildings and so many people living in one place. It was noisy and some of the streets were narrow, dark and stinking. It made me glad my home was in the hills.

The castle on the hill was an amazing sight, even if the governor refused to surrender and let us in. We were walking down Canongate towards the Palace of Holyrood, where the Prince would stay, when all of a sudden we heard gunfire.

We all scattered to the sides of the road until we realised that it was coming from the castle, and we were well out of range of their guns. I kept glancing behind me, terrified, but there were no more shots.

Father laughed and shook his head. "That's the troops defending the castle, but they'll not come after us. The town belongs to the Jacobites!" Then he turned serious. "It's the government army we need to watch out for. General Cope tried to catch us in the Highlands and failed, but we've had word that he's nearby with his army. The wind was too strong for his ships to land here in Edinburgh, but they'll get as close as they can."

"Will there be a battle, Father?" I was excited, but Father's face was grave.

"Yes, we'll have to fight them, Rob. It'll no be easy. Never take going into battle lightly. Men die in battle." He put his hand on my shoulder. "I must go now and meet with the clan chiefs, but you and Jamie stay with the men and I'll find you."

It was a night I will always remember. Jamie and I were treated like grown men. We joined in the toast to Prince Charlie's father, King James. I drank claret for the first time, a red wine smuggled into Scotland from France. My head was fair sore in the morning.

GENERAL COPE'S JOURNEY

The day after Prince Charlie and his army met at Glenfinnan, General Cope and his army set out to stop them. But the two armies missed each other and Cope took a very big detour!

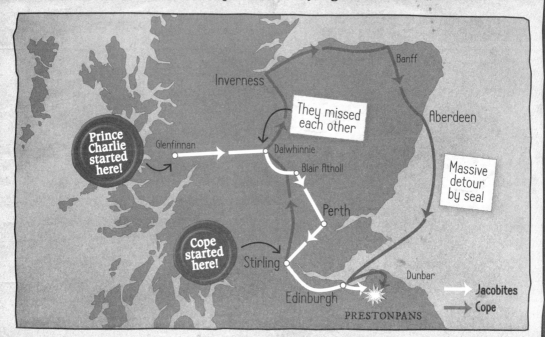

JACOBITE SYMBOLS AND CODES

The Jacobites used codes to keep their plans secret. In this letter, written to James Francis Edward Stuart in July 1715, real names were swapped for pretend ones in case the letter was read by enemies.

the lawyer =
Duke of Marlborough
(British government)

Belley =
Duke of Berwick
(Jacobite)

Talon =
Marquie de Torcy (French diplomat and a Jacobite)

Horne =
George I

I have assured **the lawyer** that none of the deeds were ever writ by **Belley** or **Talon**'s own hand... If **Horne**'s agent asks Talon any question, this latter will seem to know nothing at all of the matter, and tell him plainly that he is not to meddle.

Based on a real Jacobite letter.

The Jacobites used secret symbols and sayings to identify themselves:

The white cockade, a ribbon folded to look like petals of a rose, was the main Jacobite symbol.

Jacobites often wore tartan waistcoats.

Jacobites would raise a glass over a bowl of water and say "To the king!", secretly meaning "To the king over the water" = James VII or VIII in exile in Europe.

Some Jacobites had a secret picture of Prince Charlie in the house. It looked like a splurge of paint, but when viewed through a special metal cylinder, it revealed the face of the Prince.

Two days later we gathered outside Edinburgh and marched to fight General Cope's army. I was buzzing with excitement. The Prince looked regal in a blue coat, red waistcoat and breeches, and his blue bonnet with a white cockade. His fine broadsword gleamed in the sunlight.

We camped for the night outside Edinburgh, near the sea. I wrapped my plaid around me and started thinking about how much I missed Mother's bannocks, Aggie's teasing and wee Meggie's squeals. I even missed Granny telling me to wrap up warm.

In the middle of the night, Jamie shook me. "Wake up, Rob, but for the Prince's sake keep quiet! It's time to go."

We made our way through mists and boggy marshes in the dark to surprise Cope's army at Prestonpans. It was exciting, but as we set off every dog around started barking!

They didn't stop until we'd all crept past in the dark. I was sure Cope's soldiers would hear, even from far away.

As the first streaks of dawn light were showing we approached the government army from behind. A single cannon shot went off, harsh and loud. They had seen us!

Next came cannon fire from both sides. Caught up in the excitement of my first real battle, my heart beating fit to burst, I ran forward. I was yelling with all the other Highlanders as we charged. I held my targe up as I'd been taught and gripped my sword. I didn't have time to think about how scared I was.

The battle was short, but fierce and shocking. Our Highlanders carried long-bladed axes, dirks, swords and even pitchforks. Cope's army were trained soldiers with muskets, but they had fear on their faces when they saw us, and many turned to run. There was blood and loud screams. I saw sights I never want to see again, and I was sick to my stomach for most of it, but we won.

I'd lost sight of Jamie in the fight. "Jamie! Jamie, where are ye?" I called.

"Rob!" I heard Father shout, and there he was, with Jamie. Both were spattered with blood and covered in cuts and bruises, as was I, but we were all safe.

MERCIFUL PRINCE

Unlike government leaders, Charlie showed mercy to his opponents, because he felt responsible for all the British people. He gave two commands after winning the Battle of Prestonpans.

1. The wounded on both sides shall be cared for.
2. All the dead must be buried.

BATTLE REPORT: *Prestonpans*

When: 21st September 1745

Size of armies: Jacobites 2,000–2,500, Government 2,200–2,800

Weapons: Jacobites: muskets, broadswords, targes, axes and pitchforks! Government: cannons, mortars, muskets and bayonets.

Tactics: The Jacobites sneaked up on the government army just before dawn, then unleashed their terrifying Highland Charge.

Casualties: Jacobites 100; Government 300 killed, 1,400 captured

Outcome: The government soldiers were terrified and ran away. The Jacobites won in just 15 minutes. After that they controlled most of Scotland, and got more money and weapons from the French. The government started to take the Jacobites seriously.

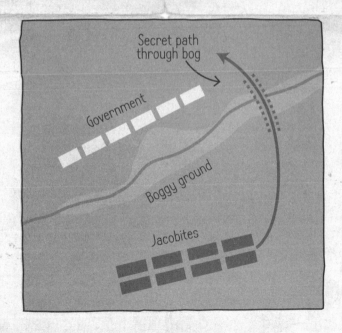

SHARING THE NEWS

In the 1700s there were no TV, radio or photographs, and newspapers weren't popular yet. Often the only pictures of famous people were funny sketches called caricatures, which were used by both sides to make the other look bad. Royal news and government messages were printed on sheets of paper called 'broadsides', which were pinned up like posters.

Believed to be a caricature of General Cope.

Abbay of Holyroodhouse, 26th September 1745.

ALL those who are willing to take Arms for Our Service as Volunteers, and to concur under Our Command, whether on Foot or Horseback, to the Deliverance of their Country, are hereby ordered to repair this Day at Two in the Afternoon to the Great Hall of this Our Palace of *Holyroodhouse*, there to have their Names enrolled.

CHARLES P. R.

Prince Charlie calls for soldiers, based on a real broadside.

Most people couldn't read, so songs were written to record history and pass it on. Armies sang marching songs to help them keep in rhythm and songs to spur them on for battle. But songs did not always tell the whole truth and were often used to mock the other side. The popular Jacobite song *Hey, Johnny Cope, are ye waking yet?* was written after the Battle of Prestonpans to make fun of General Cope. He wasn't really asleep when the battle started, but he may as well have been!

5. DANGER IN THE HIGHLANDS

AGGIE, SEPTEMBER 1745

One morning at the sheiling our neighbour Jeannie rushed up the hill in quite a state.

"I just met some cattle drovers on their way north," she gasped. "They say there's an army of government soldiers come to the Highlands. I've seen birds disturbed over the far hill, so they're likely coming up the pass."

Mother turned to me, looking serious. "Aggie, take Meggie back home as quickly as you can," she told me. "But remember, keep an eye out for the soldiers. If you see them coming, hide. Be safe, ma bairns."

"Where are you going, Mother?" I asked her.

She hesitated and then looked me straight in the eye. "You're a clever lass, Aggie. I canna tell you, then if anyone asks, you can honestly say you don't know." I knew she meant soldiers or government spies who didn't like Prince Charlie.

I strapped a basket full of food and other supplies to my back. It was heavy, but I'm quite strong. We set off, with Meggie chattering away while I kept an eye out for soldiers.

"Tuck your skirts up, Meggie, to stop them getting wet," I said as we came to the burn.

We were almost across, with our feet in the freezing water, when I saw a soldier coming up the hill. His red coat was bright against the dull bracken. I got such a fright that I almost slipped on the wet stones. He'd not seen us yet because we were hidden in a dip – but not for long.

"Meggie, a soldier's coming," I whispered, pushing her up onto the dry grass. "Run over there and hide behind those bushes. You need to be so very quiet. If I can't get away from him, go home and tell Granny. Can you do that for me?"

Meggie looked worried, but she was very brave and nodded.

"Good lass. Off you go and be quiet, like a wee mouse."

I waited till she was hidden before I stepped out of the water.

My feet were frozen, but I had other things to worry about. The soldier had seen me. He smiled as he came up to me, but I didn't trust his smile.

"Now, where are you off to?" he asked.

I tried to think of what to say, then I had an idea.

I coughed and sneezed loudly right towards him. He backed away. I sniffed and spoke in a childish voice. "Ma mither's sick. All oor family are sick but me."

I coughed again and tried to look sickly. "Could you help us, sir?"

He scowled and stepped further away from me. "What is it, this sickness?"

I sneezed at him again. "I'm just a lass, I dinnae know, but our father is already lost to us, and the babe, too."

He stepped back again. "Don't you come any nearer. I don't want your sickness!" he snarled. He set off down the hill, fast as a frightened deer, and took a huge leap over the burn.

I sat down beside my basket, smiling despite my thumping heart. I called to Meggie as soon as he was well out of sight and we set off home. Meggie and I laughed about it all the way, although I was careful to keep watch for any more soldiers.

I was glad to get back because Granny did not look well at all. I made a hot brew from some herbs and it seemed to help, and I decided to gather some heather tops to help her cough.

It was getting late and Mother was still not back. Granny told me not to fret too much as wee Meggie might get scared. So I cuddled Meggie and pulled her close.

REDCOATS

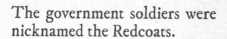

The government soldiers were nicknamed the Redcoats.

They included English and many Irish men, as well as Scottish Lowlanders and Highlanders.

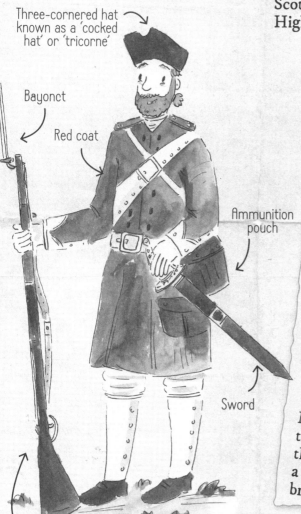

Three-cornered hat known as a 'cocked hat' or 'tricorne'

Bayonet

Red coat

Ammunition pouch

Sword

Musket

Many Highlanders supported the government and joined the Redcoat army. They wore a plaid and bonnet instead of breeches and a cocked hat.

"What are you knitting, Granny?" Meggie asked.

"A bonnet for you, lass, to keep you warm in the wintertime."

After we'd had some oatcakes and broth, I sat with Meggie to practise our reading. Mother was teaching us to read from our family Bible, as Father taught Rob. Then we carded some more wool for Granny. We sang songs together while we worked and they made me think of Father, who loves to sing. I felt close to him even though he was far away.

As it got late, I sang Meggie a lullaby and she dropped off to sleep beside me.

A GAELIC LULLABY

Aggie may have sung this old Scots Gaelic lullaby, which is still sung today.

O ba bà mo leanabh	Oh hush-a-bye, my little baby
bà mo leanabh, bà	Hush, my little baby, hush
O bà mo leanabh	Oh hush-a-bye, my little baby
nì mo leanabhs' an ba bà	My own little baby will hush-a-bye

Just then, the door of the croft rattled.

"Mother!" I ran into her arms. "You're home. I was feart the soldiers had caught you!"

"It would take more than a few soldiers to stop me coming home, Aggie."

HIGHLAND LIFE

Hen, if there were no phones, internet or TV, how did the Highlanders know what was happening in the world?

Well, cattle drovers travelled all around Britain passing gossip from place to place.

You can't beat a good blether, eh Hen?

And Jacobite women passed on top-secret messages and letters.

Were there no posties back then, Hen?

Yes, they rode horses, but the roads were bad and travelling was dangerous.

Yeah, Hen – letters sometimes got stolen by the enemy.

And only rich folk could pay someone to ride across the country with a letter!

True, Hen, and most people couldn't write anyway. Good job they liked a blether!

MULTI-TASKING

Highland women used drop spindles instead of spinning wheels, so they could spin wool while they did other jobs like caring for animals and children. Once they'd spun the wool, they knitted it or sent it to a weaver to be made into plaids.

A BATH? WHAT'S THAT?

Townships were built near a source of water, like a burn, for drinking and washing. The women and children collected drinking water, but they probably didn't bother washing themselves in the icy cold burn very often!

PARTY TIME!

Many Scottish traditions still popular today come from Highland clan culture.

- A **ceilidh** is a gathering with storytelling and singing.
- **Highland Games** were first held in the 11th century to choose the strongest clansmen and the best musicians and dancers for the chief's household.
- **Shinty** (Gaelic: *camanachd*) has been a popular ball game in the Highlands for nearly 2,000 years. It was traditionally played on feast days by many players, often for several hours.

6. THE MARCH INTO ENGLAND

ROB, NOVEMBER 1745

It was cold, but our spirits were high. Jamie and I had proven ourselves in our first battle, and now we were marching towards England.

"I heard we have 8,000 men," Jamie told me. It was more than I could count, and nothing could stop us now.

While we were in Edinburgh we'd been given extra clothes and weapons. There was enough food, biscuits and broth, but I missed Mother's stew. I often wondered how she and the lassies were faring at home. I wrote them a letter, but I didn't know when it would get there.

We marched for days, through the cold, windy weather. Sometimes we sheltered in empty barns, but mostly we slept outside wrapped in our plaids. My feet hurt and I longed to sleep in a real bed.

Six days after leaving Edinburgh we finally reached England and camped outside Carlisle, where we prepared to lay siege to the town. We dug ditches for our thirteen cannons close to the city walls. We were within range of enemy musket fire, but since we worked at night in the dark their soldiers kept missing us and no one was injured. One morning I shook Jamie awake.

"Carlisle has surrendered," I told him. "They're waving a white flag!"

The Prince ordered no looting, and we marched into Carlisle to the sound of a hundred bagpipes playing, following Prince Charlie riding on a huge white charger. Cannons and muskets were fired in salute, everyone cheered and the church bells rang. It was an amazing sight. We had taken our first town in England. Nothing could stop us now!

THE SIEGE OF CARLISLE

Instead of returning the government army's fire while they were digging at night, the Jacobite soldiers held up their bonnets on the end of their spades and laughed at them.

For the next month we marched through England in the snow. My feet were so cold I could hardly feel them, but we were on our way to London, and we would soon have a Stuart king on the throne again!

By the beginning of December, more than three months since we had left our home, we reached Derby, where we stopped for a day or two. I saw my father approaching, with a dark look on his face.

"There's been a change of plan, Rob."

"What is it?" I asked.

"We're turning back, lad. There are too many government troops between us and London, and the French army has no come to help us, as they promised. The odds are too great against us. We're going home."

"Where we should have stayed," Jock growled under his breath.

Father glared at him, and he was silent. I could tell my father wasn't pleased about the decision, but he was fiercely loyal to the Prince.

I felt crushed by the news. "But we're just six days march from London," I protested to Jock as we prepared to march back north. "We should keep going."

Jock shook his head. "It's not for us to decide, lad. We soldiers do as we're told."

Why did the Jacobites turn back, Hen?

Well, they'd expected more support from English Jacobites and a French invasion, which didn't happen.

Were they worried about facing the big government armies, with their men so exhausted from marching?

Exactly. Most of Prince Charlie's advisers wanted to head back to Scotland, where there were more supplies and men waiting to join them.

Charlie had to go then, Hen, even if he didn't want to?

That's right, but taking London was his aim. Prince Charlie wasn't happy.

PANIC IN LONDON

When Prince Charlie's army marched 200 miles into England, the British government was not prepared and it caused panic in London. George II was all ready to set sail for Europe if they had reached the capital.

JACOBITES IN MANCHESTER

300 Manchester men enlisted to form their own regiment within Bonnie Prince Charlie's army. But when he was forced to retreat to Scotland, the Manchester Regiment stayed at Carlisle as a rearguard.

It was five days before Christmas, on the Prince's 25th birthday, when we reached the River Esk, north of Carlisle. We only had to cross it and we'd be back in Scotland, but the rain had been pouring down on us and now the river was a torrent.

The cavalry was sent in first, just above the ford, to form a barrier against the swirling water. We each grabbed the neck of the next man's coat, and formed a huge line of men crossing the river. At one point only our heads were above the water, but we held on and kept moving across. I glanced

back and saw that the river was filled with line after line of
men slowly moving to the other side.

We all climbed out soaked and weary, but the pipers
struck up a jig and we danced and cheered until our clothes
were almost dry. We were delighted to be back in Scotland.

By the time we reached Glasgow, our clothes were little more than rags. But there something amazing happened. Prince Charlie had ordered a new coat, bonnet, waistcoat, two shirts, a pair of stockings and new shoes for each of us.

"Can ye believe it, Jamie? Don't we look grand."

"Aye, Rob."

"Come on, lads," Father said, in his new tartan waistcoat. "The Prince wants to inspect his men on Glasgow Green. Let's be off."

We set off from Glasgow with a spring in our step. We were heading to Stirling to take the castle, but the government forces were camped on the way, at Falkirk, and we would have to fight them.

The weather was foul but the wind was behind us as we set out for battle from the summit on Falkirk Muir. The government troops started up the steep hill as rain and wind blew straight into their faces, probably making their gunpowder damp, too.

"It's their dragoons!" Jamie yelled.

We charged towards them, firing our muskets then dropping them as we'd done before. I held up my targe and ran at them with my sword.

The battle was fierce, but they struggled to come up the hill towards us and many of their men fell. As daylight faded, the government troops retreated, and we chased them into Falkirk as they ran. The Jacobites had won, and Jamie, Father and I had all survived another battle.

BATTLE REPORT: *Falkirk*

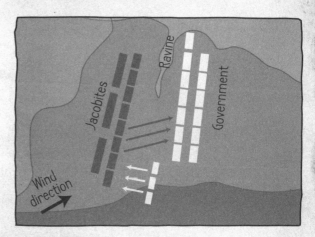

When: 17th January 1746

Size of armies: Jacobites 7,800, Government 7,200

Tactics: The Jacobites climbed the hill in better weather then used their Highland charge. The government army were forced to attack uphill in wind and rain.

Casualties:
Government 300 killed, 300 captured; Jacobites fewer

Outcome: The government army's gunpowder got wet and their cannons got stuck in a bog. Their dragoons struggled up the hill towards Jacobite musket fire then the deadly Highland charge. The victory gave the Jacobites a boost, but the government's huge army had now returned from fighting in Europe.

DID SOMEONE SAY DRAGONS?

Not dragons – *dragoons* – a name used for soldiers mounted on horseback, also called *cavalry*.

THE SIEGE OF STIRLING CASTLE

After the Battle of Falkirk, the Jacobites tried to capture Stirling Castle, the ancestral home of the Stuart kings. However, their attempt failed and after less than two weeks, they headed north to take back Inverness.

FACT-TASTIC FACT

ROB AND AGGIE'S CROFT

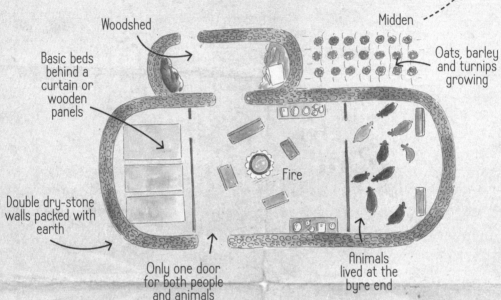

Woodshed

Basic beds behind a curtain or wooden panels

Midden

Oats, barley and turnips growing

Double dry-stone walls packed with earth

Fire

Only one door for both people and animals

Animals lived at the byre end

No chimney – smoke filtered out through the thatch. Soot made the inside walls black – they were called 'blackhouses'

Wooden rafters covered with thatch made of turf and reeds/straw

Very small windows

Bare flagstones or packed earth – no tiles or carpet

Wooden stools, benches and chairs

Partition between people and animals

7. 1746, AT HOME IN THE HIGHLANDS

AGGIE, FEBRUARY 1746

I'm glad it is almost spring, although it's still bitterly cold. This winter has been the worst I can remember, and we are very hungry. The deep snow means we can hardly go out foraging. In December Granny turned very sick, and none of my special drinks, herbs and poultices seemed to help.

"Aggie," Mother said one night when Granny was very weak, "sometimes when people are older, their bodies canna work hard enough to make them better."

"I know, Mother." I bit my lip, trying hard not to cry.

Mother drew me in close. "Aggie, you're a wonderful lass. Granny told me she's so proud of you and all you've learned about healing. She is tired now, and it's her time. She won't last much longer, but she doesn't want you to feel too sad when she's gone." Mother hugged me tightly. "Go and say goodbye to her now. It's all right to cry, but give her your best smile, too."

The house seemed so much quieter after Granny died. Meggie cried a lot, but I taught her how to make little wraps of the scented herbs Granny loved, and that seemed to help.

Then one morning, when Mother was out, I heard Meggie calling me from the byre end of the croft. "Aggie, come quickly! It's Nan!"

Nan was our goat. She was having twins and I knew from Meggie's squeal that they were about to be born. Meggie and

I sat beside her and I stroked her back. The first kid arrived soon after.

"Why isn't it moving?" Meggie asked.

I rubbed it fiercely with some straw and when it started to move I cleared its nose and mouth. "There, it's fine now, Meggie."

I put it beside Nan, who licked its face but then moved away as the second kid was born. I rubbed it and placed it close to its mother and brother. Soon they were happily settled and having their first feed. "Don't they look braw, Aggie. Let's call that one Rob," Meggie giggled, pointing at the one with the black patch over its eye.

We found it hard to get everything done on the croft over winter without our menfolk, and I wished every day that Father and Rob would come home. We heard news that the army was back in Scotland, but we didn't know if Father and Rob were safe. They might be injured, or worse. I didn't dare think of that.

One day I was busy chopping wood for the fire (I was getting very good at it) when I heard Meggie shouting. I dropped the axe and raced off to see what was wrong.

"It canna be!" I heard Mother cry out.

Heart thumping, I stopped, hardly able to breathe.

Three bedraggled men stood there and it took me a moment to realise it was Father, Rob and another lad. I couldn't get my feet to move fast enough. They were home!

"This is my friend Jamie," Rob said, when he could get a word in. The other lad smiled, a little nervous at the fuss we were all making.

"Welcome, Jamie," Mother said. "Come inside, all of you."

A HIGHLAND MENU

blackberries

raspberries

Menu

breakfast

porridge with foraged berries, nettles, hazelnuts or beechnuts

lunch

foraged dandelion, wild mushroom and wild garlic soup

goat's cheese or curd cheese with oatcakes or bannocks

dinner

turnip, wild parsnip and barley stew

black pudding

hazelnuts

beechnuts

nettles

goat's cheese with bannocks

These were cooked on a girdle iron over the fire. There were no ovens to bake bread.

dandelions

mushrooms

parsnips

Animals were too precious to kill, so Highlanders ate very little meat, but animals were sometimes bled a little to make black pudding.

wild garlic

They put their packs down and warmed their hands at the fire. Hot soup was bubbling in the pot and they ate it with the last of the day's oatcakes. Mother told them about Granny, and we all shared our memories of her as we ate. Mother looked happier than she had for a long time, as she listened to Father and Rob.

She peered at Father across the fire. "Where is the Prince now?"

"He's safe, but did ye hear how they tried to catch him and were chased off by Lady Anne?"

Mother grinned. "Is that so?"

"Aye! The Prince got away just in time."

"How did it happen, Father?" I asked, keen to hear the story.

He put another log on the fire and started his tale. "The Prince was staying with Lady Anne Mackintosh at Moy. She was warned that government troops were coming to capture him, so she sent the Prince off in the middle of the night – with his bonnet on top of his nightcap!"

I giggled, but Rob frowned at me and Father continued.

"Then Lady Anne sent the blacksmith and four others to wait for the government's men, all 1,500 of them!"

Mother and I gasped.

"The men of Moy made a lot of noise, shouting clan war cries and firing a few shots. The enemy, fearing that all of the Prince's army was there, turned back to Inverness then fled to the far north. Hundreds have deserted the government army since then to come and join us."

"When we captured Inverness, the Prince said we could go and see our families," Rob told us.

"The Duke of Cumberland 's leading the government army now, though. He's brought more troops back from the war in France, and they're heading north from London. That'll no be an easy fight." Father looked anxious.

"Well, that's a worry for another day," Mother said brightly. "You're here now."

Jamie was sitting quietly, his flop of dark hair falling over his eyes. "Are you not visiting your family, Jamie?" I asked.

"They're over by Aberdeen. It's too far," he said quietly.

"Well, you're always welcome here, lad," Mother told him, filling up his bowl again.

'COLONEL ANNE'
(1723–1784)

LADY ANNE MACKINTOSH

Anne Mackintosh, aged 22, rode out on her horse, carrying a pair of pistols, to raise her clansmen to fight for the Jacobites – even though her husband, the clan chief, was a captain in the government army. After two weeks she had a regiment of 300 men, who joined Prince Charlie's army at the Battle of Falkirk. Women did not fight on the battlefield but they helped in lots of other ways. Anne Mackintosh welcomed the Prince and his men to stay at her home. When government troops came to capture them in the night, she tricked them with just a few men. The next month her husband was captured by the Jacobites and put into his wife's custody. Prince Charlie said, "He could not be in better security."

It was soon time for them to head back to Inverness to prepare for battle with the Duke of Cumberland's army. I was scared we'd never see them again.

"Be careful, and burn the letters we sent you," Father told us. "There are Redcoats all around. If they find that you support the Prince, they will be very cruel."

"We'll come back as soon as we can," Rob said as he hugged Mother. I stood outside and watched them walk away until I could see them no more.

MISSING TREASURE

In March 1746 a ship carrying supplies for the Jacobites from French King Louis XV, including £13,000 in gold — worth about £1.5 million today! — was captured and stolen. Rumours say that some of the gold might still be hidden in the Highlands!

THE DUKE OF CUMBERLAND
(1721–1765)

- The Duke of Cumberland was the third son of King George II.

- His full name was **Prince William Augustus, Duke of Cumberland.** He was nicknamed **Sweet William** by his followers and **The Butcher** by the Jacobites.

DUKE OF CUMBERLAND

- He was an experienced army general, and was Commander-in-Chief of the British, German, Austrian and Dutch troops in their war against France.

- In January 1746, he turned his attention to stopping the Jacobite rebellion.

THE BUILD-UP TO BATTLE...

The Redcoats

After losing again at Falkirk, the government had to take the Jacobites more seriously. **The Duke of Cumberland** took over command of the army. He had the power, money and experience to provide food, weapons and training. He arrived in Scotland in early 1746 and headed for Aberdeen, where he taught his soldiers **new battle tactics** to defeat the Jacobites' terrifying Highland charge, including:

Bayonets fixed to Brown Bess muskets around the gun barrel. This new development allowed soldiers to shoot, then immediately stab, instead of stopping to screw on their bayonets.

Volley firing – lines of soldiers took turns to fire their muskets, then reload, so there was no break in their attack.

The Jacobites

The Jacobites weren't so well prepared. After the long march into England and the Battle of Falkirk, many Highlanders had gone home for a rest, and others were away fighting in the far north. When they arrived at Culloden the army did not have enough weapons or food, and Prince Charlie and his senior officers did not agree on tactics...

LETTERS FROM CULLODEN

Based on real soldiers' letters.

I've never been so cold or hungry in my life. I've not had a meal in days. I can't remember the last time I slept in a bed! The men have had enough. We marched all the way to Derby only to turn and march back. I've heard talk of us marching right through to Nairn. That's 12 miles away! We're exhausted. I just want to sleep and eat. I want to go home.

James MacDonald

JACOBITE SOLDIER

The men are tired and hungry. They need rest. A 12 mile march tonight would be stupid. Half the men are missing anyway – gone to find something to eat so they don't starve. I say we wait here and fight tomorrow!

John o'Sullivan

JACOBITE OFFICER

Dear Molly,

We have these rebels on the run now! Our new General, the Duke of Cumberland, is a great man. He's taught us new ways of fighting these Highlanders. We all feel a bit more confident in battle these days. As I write it is the Duke's birthday and he's given us cheese, bread, meat and wine! We're well looked after and we're ready to fight tomorrow. I cannot see how we can fail.

See you soon,

Callum

GOVERNMENT ARMY OFFICER

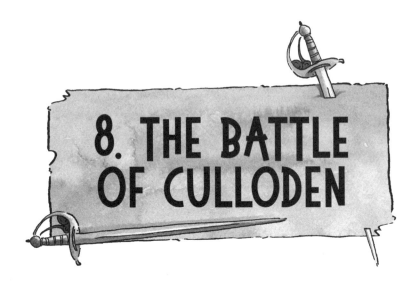

8. THE BATTLE OF CULLODEN

ROB, APRIL 1746

We were camped out on the moors near Culloden, preparing to fight the Duke of Cumberland's army. With so many enemies around us, supplies were not getting through. There wasn't enough food to go round and we were all starving.

"Wake up, Rob!" Jamie shook me. "It's morning. Let's go and find something to eat."

I scrambled to my feet, wiping the sleep from my eyes and shivering. It was freezing cold and the rain had

turned to sleet. I gathered my plaid tighter around me.
A few of us decided to go and hunt for food. Father was
away with another regiment, and I convinced myself he'd be
pleased when we brought back a rabbit or two.

We left the camp and hunted for hours, but by late
afternoon we'd only caught one scrawny hare. It was barely
enough to feed two, and there were four of us. I was left with
a roaring belly. When we got back to camp, the others were
packing up. Father was back and not too happy.

"Rob, Jamie, where did you lads go? I've been looking for you." I felt bad that we'd not brought back anything for Father to eat, especially when he shared his last two oatcakes with us, leaving himself with a small lump of hard bread.

"We're going to surprise them, like we did at Prestonpans," Father told us. "They've been celebrating the Duke of Cumberland's birthday, so they'll no be ready for a fight."

We marched through the night, we Highlanders at the front and the Prince and other regiments following behind. It was twelve miles over rough ground to the government camp at Nairn. We had to stay quiet so they would not hear us approach. The moon was high in the sky when we were told to halt. I heard the sound of a drum beating in the distance.

YOUNG COMMANDERS

Both the Duke of Cumberland and Prince Charlie were only 25 years old when they led their armies at the Battle of Culloden. They were distant cousins.

"No! That's the Duke's army," Father said, shaking his head. "They're awake. It's not going to work."

He was right: word came that we were to turn back, and that some behind us already had. As we retreated, tired and hungry, I felt as if my heart was sinking along with my boots into the soggy marsh. If we'd had any energy, we'd have started fighting amongst ourselves. Dawn had broken when we were at last allowed to stop. I was asleep before I touched the ground, and I didn't care how cold it was.

Before I knew it we were roused and told to prepare for battle: Cumberland's troops had already arrived to fight us here on Culloden Moor! I was shivering and so hungry it felt like my bones were knocking together. We were passed a small piece of hard bread each, hardly enough to feed a bairn.

"Rob," Jamie called to me, "today we'll fight for the Prince, and we will win!"

I turned towards him and saw that he was tired and hungry, but he had a proud grin on his face. With my plaid over my shoulder I pulled on my blue bonnet and lifted my sword. "Aye, we will win. I can feel it, too." I slung on my musket, checked I had my pouch of ammunition, and tucked my pistol in my belt. I was ready, but secretly I had a dark fear grabbing my belly that I had never felt before.

An icy mist hung close to the battlefield. Jamie was by me and I could see Father ahead. He looked for me and nodded.

The snow and rain stung like icy needles as the government army arrived with their cocked hats, long red coats and white breeches. There were Highlanders in that army, too. I'd heard that some wanted to get revenge on their neighbours for old arguments. I could feel my blood rising as I scrugged my bonnet down over my forehead and looked round at the Jacobite army readying for battle.

There was the noise of men and horses, and the sound of pipes and drums. Then our cannons roared, and theirs returned fire. Smoke stung the back of my throat. The battle had begun and we waited for the command, drumming up our courage. I wondered if our commanders could see in the heavy rain and sleet.

At last the command came and we surged forward, yelling our battle cries and stumbling over the marshy ground. We had to run a long way, as we were farthest from the enemy. So many of our brave men were being cut down by musket and cannon fire. I tried not to look.

I don't remember much except swinging my sword even though my arms ached, and the cries of my friends as they fell. The call went up to retreat. We had lost.

I ran with those who could still run, and saw Jamie staggering. He was bleeding badly and hardly able to stand, so I grabbed his arm and swung it over my shoulder. We stumbled off that dreadful Culloden Moor, leaving so many of our men dead or dying. The government troops were chasing fast behind, killing those who lay wounded. Seeing that horror gave us strength to keep going. We had to get away.

THE BUTCHER

After the Battle of Culloden, the Duke of Cumberland ordered his army to shoot the retreating Jacobites and kill the wounded where they lay. They captured or killed as many Jacobites as they could find.

PIPING-HOT WEAPONS

Until 1996 the bagpipes were classed as a weapon of war. James Reid, one of several pipers at the Battle of Culloden, was tried for high treason in England. Reid claimed that he was innocent because he carried no weapon on the battlefield, only his bagpipes. However, as Highland regiments were always led into battle by pipers, the judges ruled that bagpipes were an instrument of war. James Reid was found guilty, and was hung, drawn and quartered.

BATTLE REPORT: *Culloden*

When: 16th April 1746

Size of armies: Jacobites 5,500, Government 7,500

Weapons: Jacobites: 12 cannon, muskets, swords and targes; Government: many cannon, mortars, lots of cavalry, muskets with new fixed bayonets.

Tactics: Jacobites: the Highland charge; Government: more men, more powerful weapons.

What went wrong for the Jacobites?

- They didn't have enough food, so they wanted to fight quickly.
- They tried to attack at night, but their plan failed.
- They were starving and exhausted when the government army arrived mid morning ready to fight.
- The battlefield was boggy, slowing down the Highland charge.

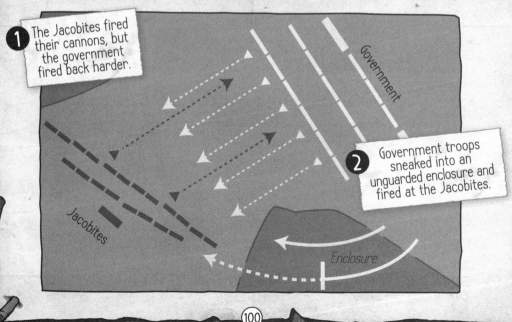

1 The Jacobites fired their cannons, but the government fired back harder.

2 Government troops sneaked into an unguarded enclosure and fired at the Jacobites.

Government

Jacobites

Enclosure

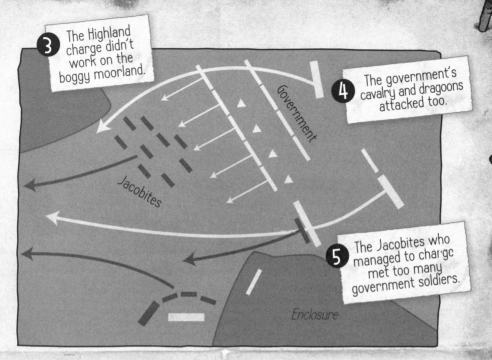

3 The Highland charge didn't work on the boggy moorland.

4 The government's cavalry and dragoons attacked too.

5 The Jacobites who managed to charge met too many government soldiers.

Government

Jacobites

Enclosure

Casualties: Jacobites 1,200 killed, 1,200 wounded; Government 50 killed, 300 wounded

THE END OF THE RISING

Prince Charlie still had men, but his army had no weapons or food. His only option was to flee back to France. The '45 Rising, and the Jacobite Cause, were over.

THE LAST BATTLE

Culloden was the last major battle fought on British soil.

9. HIDING FROM THE REDCOATS

AGGIE, APRIL 1746

I still have nightmares about the day soldiers came to our croft.
We'd heard that the battle near Inverness had gone badly
and many had died. Now the Redcoats were searching for
any Jacobite soldiers or supporters they could find. Wee Meggie
and I were huddled at the back of the woodshed under some
torn tattie bags, piles of peat and damp old straw. It was dark
and fousty, and I could feel tiny beasties nipping at my bare arms
and legs, but I couldn't swat them away in case I made a noise.

"Make not a sound, and do not come out until night falls, no matter what you hear, Mary Agnes," Mother had warned me. She only calls me by my full name when I'm in trouble, but this was different: she was deadly serious.

Mother looked as if she was going to cry as she hugged us close and made us promise to do as she asked. "If I don't come for you by dawn," she said, "head up to the sheiling and wait for me there."

After a while, we heard soldiers' heavy boots and their rough voices shouting at Mother, asking where Father was and if she was hiding any Jacobite traitors. Meggie held my hand tightly and I hugged her and covered her ears. I hoped she couldn't feel me shaking.

One of the soldiers tugged at the shed door and pulled it off its hinges. The bright sunlight dazzled me. He poked about the logs and knocked over the pile of peat stacks. I held my breath and screwed my eyes tight shut, hoping Meggie wouldn't start to cry. My heart was beating so hard I was sure he'd hear it.

Then he left, shouting to the others that there was no one there.

We waited with cramped legs, shivering with cold, until the last of the sunlight crept across the log pile. I pushed aside the straw and left Meggie sleeping while I had a look around.

The house was a mess: everything was broken, and Mother was nowhere to be found. I heard a footstep outside and froze, hardly daring to breathe. I prayed that Meggie would stay sleeping as I leant back into the shadows.

Another footstep. I held my breath, biting my lip as I saw a shadow cross the doorway. A head peered inside.

A soft, familiar voice said my name: "Aggie? Is that you?"

I gasped and rushed to my brother. "Rob!" I sobbed. "It's you, Rob. I was so scared."

We heard Meggie crying, and as we ran out to her I noticed that Rob was limping. Meggie's wee face crumpled as she reached out her arms to me, but then she saw Rob and gave him a huge smile.

"Is Father no with you, Rob?" I asked, terrified of the answer.

Rob shook his head. "He's with the Prince, Aggie. He sent me home because of my leg, and to make sure you were all right. Where's Mother?"

Early the next morning, Mother staggered back. She'd hurt her foot, but she told us she was fine. She was so happy that we were all safe. She'd escaped from the soldiers, then hidden from them in the hills.

"I met two of our soldiers hiding in the hills. They were wounded and hungry, so I took them to the sheiling. I need to take them some food."

"Mother, sit down by the fire, beside Rob and Meggie," I told her. "I'll make a poultice to stop your foot bleeding, and I'll take the food up to the sheiling. You can hardly walk." I could tell she didn't want to agree, but when she tried to stand up she almost couped over onto the ground. I packed my sack with what food we could spare.

"If you see soldiers, hide from them," Mother told me. "But if they find you, tell them you're looking for a missing sheep." She hugged me tight.

HIDEY HOOPS

After Culloden, Jacobite soldier Robbie Strange fled to his girlfriend's house in Edinburgh, where he hid in the attic for several months. One day, a group of Redcoats came to search the house, but Robbie was downstairs and had no time to get up to the attic! Bella sat down at her spinning wheel and Robbie dived underneath her huge hooped petticoat. As Bella sat calmly spinning, the Redcoats ransacked the house, but they didn't think to look under a lady's skirt! Robbie and Bella were later married and lived long and happy lives.

FACT-TASTIC FACT

I hid the sack under my arisaid and set off. It was still cold on the hills and my feet were soon frozen. I hadn't gone far when I saw some Redcoats coming over the track. I ducked down under some bushes, hoping my shivering wouldn't give me away. I covered myself with snow and looked at the path behind me, thankful that it was rocky so I'd not left footprints. Rob and I used to play at hiding, so I knew I was good at it, but this was no game.

One of the soldiers stopped close to my hiding place to pee. I was terrified he would turn round and see me. I couldn't breathe, I was so scared.

They carried on, and I let them get well away before I crawled out and went on up through the hills to the sheiling. It was tucked amongst bushes and trees in a fold of the hillside.

I sang the song our father always sang us: the secret signal that I was a friend. One of the soldiers was guarding the doorway. He held up his hand to silence me, scanned the hills for Redcoats, then brought me inside.

"I'm Aggie," I told him. "My mother sent me with food."

"Your mother's a good woman," one of the men said, biting into a bannock.

They ate the food so quickly, they must have been starving. I set to work making a balm for their wounds, and a brew of herbs to help with fever.

PLANT POWER

The Highlanders lived off the land and used the plants around them however they could. They used...

- Moss for mopping up liquid, and straining milk or murky water.

- Peppermint to treat wind (yes, we do mean farts).

- Thistles as an antibiotic.

- Heather for mattresses, to make brushes and brooms, and to weave into baskets and mats.

That night, as I sat at home by the fire with my family, I thought about how much I missed Father.

"Where's your friend Jamie?" I asked Rob.

His eyes fell as he spoke. "So many were lost, it was terrible. And Jamie…" He stopped and turned away.

"Jamie's dead?" I could hardly believe it.

"Aye. I tried to help him, but he was too badly hurt." Rob wiped his hand across his eyes.

"I'm sorry, Rob. But Father will be fine. Just you wait and see." I don't know if I said that to cheer him up or because I couldn't imagine Father not coming home.

SECRET CHAMBERS

In the ancient medieval tower at Drum Castle in Aberdeenshire, hidden behind the library bookshelves, are two secret chambers. Legend says that Jacobite Alexander Irvine, the 17th Laird of Drum, hid there for three years, helped by his sister, after escaping from the Battle of Culloden.

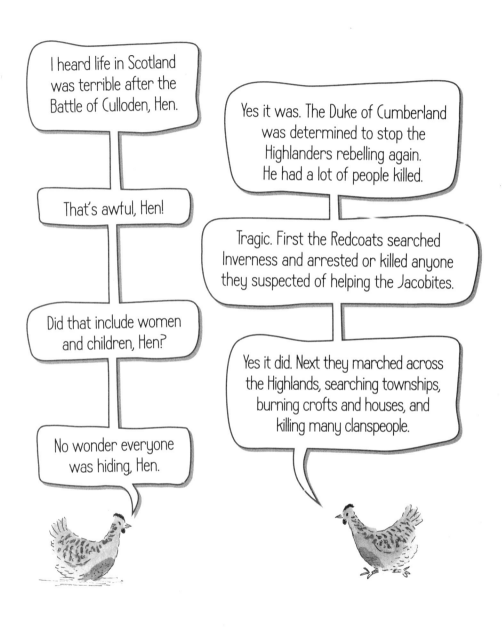

JACOBITE SONGS

Many songs were written about the Jacobites and Bonnie Prince Charlie, both at the time of the Risings and afterwards, in Gaelic, Scots and English.

Will Ye No Come Back Again?

Bonnie Charlie's noo awa,
Safely owre the friendly main;
Mony a heart will break in twa
Should he ne'er come back again.

Will ye no come back again?
Will ye no come back again?
Better lo'ed ye canna be,
Will ye no come back again?

Ye trusted in your Hielan men,
They trusted you, dear Chairlie.
They kent your hidin in the glen,
Death or exile bravin.

We watched thee in the gloamin hour,
We watched thee in the mornin grey,
Tho thirty thousand pound they gie,
O, there is nane that wad betray!

Sweet the laverock's note and lang,
liltin wildly up the glen.
But aye tae me he sings ae song,
Will ye no come back again?

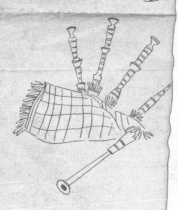

Written by Caroline Oliphant, Lady Nairne (1766–1845). Her songs were very popular during her lifetime, but she published them anonymously to hide the fact that she was a woman.

The Skye Boat Song

Speed, bonnie boat, like a bird on the wing,
Onward! the sailors cry;
Carry the lad that's born to be King
Over the sea to Skye.

Loud the winds howl, loud the waves roar,
Thunderclaps rend the air;
Baffled, our foes stand by the shore,
Follow they will not dare.

Many's the lad, fought in that day
Well the claymore did wield;
When the night came, silently lay
Dead on Culloden's field.

Though the waves leap, soft shall ye sleep,
Ocean's a royal bed.
Rocked in the deep, Flora will keep
Watch by your weary head.

Burned are their homes, exile and death
Scatter the loyal men;
Yet ere the sword cool in the sheath
Charlie will come again.

This famous song was written by Englishman Sir Harold Boulton (1859–1935) long after the Jacobite Risings.

10. THE ESCAPE OF BONNIE PRINCE CHARLIE

AGGIE, SEPTEMBER 1746

The summer of 1746 was the hardest of my life. Rob hid in the sheiling with the other two men. He was still there by September, five months later. I'd gone to the sheiling a few times with food and clothes, but Rob and the other men had to move further away because the hills were now swarming with Redcoats. We had no idea where he was, and we had no idea if Father was alive or dead.

We barely had enough to eat. When the soldiers came back looking for hidden Jacobites, Mother gave them food so they wouldn't harm us. We heard stories of terrible things happening to our neighbours.

Then one day we heard heavy footsteps outside. Mother was trying to hide Meggie and me when the door of the croft flew open and a man fell through it. I screamed, but Mother stood like she was made of stone, her hand at her mouth. She gave a strange cry and then rushed over to him.

It was Father! He was thin and dirty and dressed in rags, and he had terrible wounds, but he was alive.

"Aggie, put a pot of water on the fire," Mother told me. "Quickly now, and close the door." We helped Father to the bed. I carried over a bowlful of boiled water so Mother could bathe his wounds with rags. I put some toadflax in to help the healing, then I made broth with barley and milk. Mother had to help him sip it.

Father seemed to get worse so I made a salve for his wounds and some yarrow tea to treat his fever. He tossed about and shouted as he slept. Then one day he woke without a fever, and after that he slowly started to get well again.

Meggie and I watched the path each day so we could warn Mother if soldiers came.

"Did ye see Prince Charlie, Father?" I asked one night as we sat by the fire. "Can you tell me how he got away?"

"Aye, lass, I was on the run with him after the battle, dodging the Redcoats. He left the mainland in a boat from Borradale ten days after the battle, late at night, with five loyal men and seven boatmen."

"Did you see him again?" I asked.

"Well, at first I thought no one would ever see him again, Aggie. The night he sailed to the Western Isles there was a fierce storm, with thunder like the sky was breaking apart. I was feart that they would be lost to the waves or broken against the rocks. But I later heard they had arrived safely on Benbecula. Sometimes the Prince's only shelter was a cave, and once he had to slide on his belly to hide in a tiny hut." Father shook his head at that indignity. "Many folk don't want to be caught helping the Jacobites. I don't blame them. I didnae want to abandon him until I knew he was safely away to France."

"So where were you, Father?"

"I was busy keeping ahead of the Redcoats who were hunting us. It was no easy task. And I didn't see the Prince again until he reached Skye, almost two months later."

"How did the Prince get to Skye?"

Father paused for a moment as he tried to remember the full story. "Well, this is how the Prince told it to me:"

"One day on South Uist, a young woman called Flora MacDonald came to his aid. She dressed him like her servant, as a disguise, and gave him the name Betty Burke. The cap itched something terrible! He wished for a pistol, but Flora said it would give them away if they were caught, so she gave him a cudgel to hide in his skirts."

"They sailed at night, and the crossing was long. The Prince offered to take the oars if the boatmen were struggling."

"They arrived in the north of Skye, where they enjoyed a small feast of bread and butter, and water that poured from the cliff above."

"After another short boat ride, they walked towards their lodgings on Skye. The country people who saw them were astonished at the strange manly behaviour of Miss Flora's maid!"

"Was it soon after that he sailed for France, Father?"

"No, lass, that was weeks later in September."

"What did you do all that time?" Mother asked, as fascinated as I was.

"We kept running and hiding and keeping watch for soldiers. When we heard the ships were waiting for the Prince at Loch Nan Uamh, we made our way there. I watched him sail back to France. He told me that he hoped to return if he could get French support for the Cause.

"How were you wounded, Father?" I asked.

"I was on my way home with four other Jacobites when we were ambushed. They shot one man dead and wounded another. Then all five of them fell upon us with swords. We were outnumbered, but we managed to fight them off. In the end, only one other man was left, and he died in my arms soon after. But he told me he was proud to have helped the Prince, as was I."

A BONNIE REWARD

The British government put out a £30,000 reward – about £3 million today! – for anyone who captured Charlie, but no one came forward.

CLUNY'S CAGE

After Culloden, clan chief Cluny Macpherson's house was burned down. He hid high up on Ben Alder in a tiny cave hidden by a fallen tree, which became known as Cluny's Cage. Prince Charlie stayed there with him for two weeks. After the Prince escaped to France, Cluny stayed in the cave for eight years waiting for him to return and start another Rising, which of course he never did. Cluny Macpherson was the inspiration for a character in Robert Louis Stevenson's novel, *Kidnapped*.

BRAVE FLORA

Flora MacDonald was 24 when she took Prince Charlie by rowing boat from South Uist to Skye. She was arrested and briefly imprisoned in the Tower of London. She later emigrated to North America with her husband.

FLORA MACDONALD

BONNIE PRINCE CHARLIE'S ESCAPE ROUTE

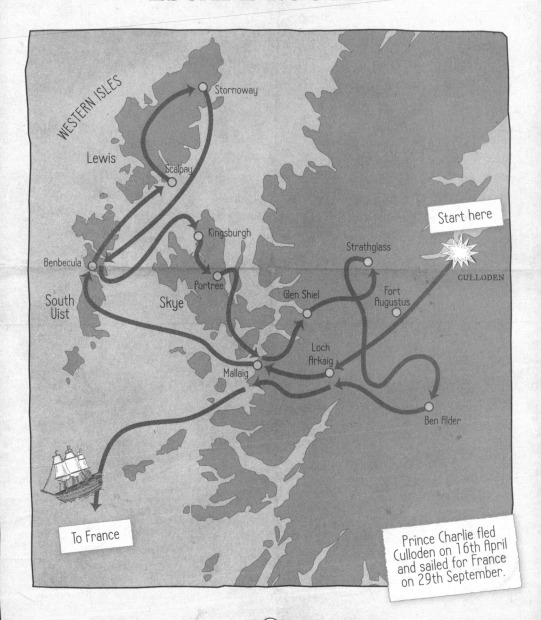

WESTERN ISLES

Lewis

Stornoway

Scalpay

Kingsburgh

Benbecula

South Uist

Portree

Skye

Start here

CULLODEN

Strathglass

Glen Shiel

Fort Augustus

Loch Arkaig

Mallaig

Ben Alder

To France

Prince Charlie fled Culloden on 16th April and sailed for France on 29th September.

WHAT HAPPENED TO BONNIE PRINCE CHARLIE?

Charles Edward Stuart spent the rest of his life living in exile, mostly in Florence and Rome. He had a daughter, Charlotte, with his Scottish partner Clementina Walkinshaw who he met during the '45 Rising. But he never recovered from the failure of the Jacobite Cause.

BONNIE PRINCE CHARLIE IN 1775

CLEMENTINA WALKINSHAW

When Charles' father died in 1766, the Pope did not support Charles as the rightful king of Britain and Ireland. He died of a stroke in Rome in 1788, aged 67, and is buried alongside his father, brother and mother in St Peter's Basilica in the Vatican.

11. MOVING ON

ROB, AUTUMN 1746

I'd been hiding in the hills for weeks, sometimes alone, sometimes with fellow soldiers. We had little to eat, surviving on water from the burns and not much else. There were fewer Redcoats than before and I could not hide forever, so I decided it was time to go home. It would be hard without Father, but I had lost all hope that he was alive.

I stood for a while looking down on the thatched roofs of our township. I was home. There was wee Meggie chasing the chickens, and Aggie chopping wood. She looked up.

"Rob! It's you, Rob! Mother, it's Rob!" Aggie came scrambling up the hill, with Meggie close behind her.

I couldn't stop the tears streaming down my face. I was so happy to see them again, even though Aggie almost knocked me over.

My one good leg was not quite steady. We stumbled down towards the croft, shouting and laughing. I was so happy that at first I didn't see Father standing with Mother, as happy a sight as I could ever imagine.

That day was a good one. For a while, Father and I sat quietly outside together, just the two of us. We shared stories of the friends we had lost and the horrors we had seen.

"Will the Prince come back again?" I asked.

Father shook his head. "I fear we'll no see him again. He said he would try, but he won't be able to raise an army. The Redcoats are executing any they can prove to be Jacobites and shipping the rest off to America or the West Indies."

"Aye, Father, we're the lucky ones."

"I've not said much to the girls yet, but things here are changing, and we need to change with them. It's not safe here for the likes of us. We'll need to leave the Highlands soon. But at least you are home, Rob, so we will all be together."

To all those dwelling in the *Highlands of Scotland*, we hereby order that:

All property of Rebel clans, including land, houses and cattle, shall be confiscated.

All Rebels found guilty shall be executed.

All suspended Rebels shall be shipped to work as slaves in our colonies.

Clan chiefs shall no longer command their people, who shall obey His Majesty's laws.

No Highlanders shall carry weapons, play the bagpipes or wear the plaid – on pain of death.

By order of His Majesty King George II

AGGIE, AUTUMN 1746

"What will we do now?" Mother asked that night as we sat by the fire. I wasn't ready for what Father said next.

"I've heard that there are ships leaving for the Americas," he said. For the first time since he'd come back, there was light in his eyes, a kind of excitement. "One of the men I met on Skye said we could farm sea kelp there for a while, until we can gain passage across the sea."

I felt as if a great hand had clutched my insides. "Across the sea... How far away is it, Father?"

He smiled. "It's a long way, Aggie. We'll all have to be brave about leaving Scotland forever, but we could start a new life there."

"We'll have to walk a long way to get to the islands, and there are still soldiers looking for Jacobites like us," Mother said, worried.

"I've spent a lot of time avoiding them, so has Father," Rob said. "We can do it."

THE HIGHLAND CLEARANCES

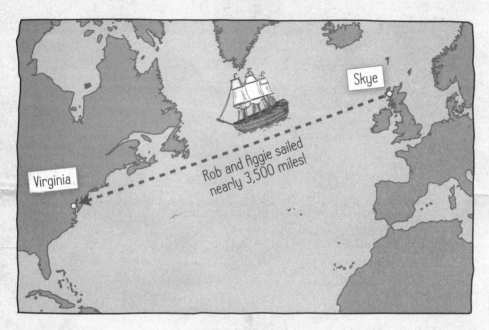

Skye

Virginia

Rob and Aggie sailed nearly 3,500 miles!

After Culloden, people started to leave the Highlands in what became known as the Highland Clearances. Rob and Aggie may have gone to live in South Carolina or Virginia.

FROM THE HIGHLANDS TO THE WILD WEST

During the Highland Clearances, lots of Scottish cattle drovers went to America where they eventually became cowboys in the Wild West.

We started preparing to leave our home behind forever. I made a pretty wreath of flowers and leaves to lay on Granny's grave. I collected some herbs and flowers to take with me, too, and packed them all carefully.

"What do you think it will be like in the Americas, Rob?" I asked.

"I don't know, Aggie. I think it might be very different from here. Are you feart of crossing the sea to get there? I think Meggie is!"

I grinned. "I think it will be the greatest adventure, Rob. All of it."

"I think you're right, Aggie." He tussled my hair as if I was as young as Meggie, but for once I just laughed.

The very next morning we were ready. Everyone but Meggie carried baskets on our backs, with everything we had in the world inside and some food for our journey.

I turned to look back at the sadly empty croft where I had lived since I was born. I had no idea what adventures lay in store for us, or what the future would bring. We were going far away across the sea to a strange land. But we were all together and that was the most important thing of all.

SOLDIER ON

With their traditional way of life destroyed, and most of their cattle confiscated, the remaining clanspeople had to find new ways to make a living. The British government began to recruit lots of soldiers from the Highlands and Islands.

HIGHLAND FORTS

Three main army garrisons were built by the British government during the Jacobite Risings to control Highland clans:

- **Fort William** (Gaelic name: *An Gearasdan* = The Garrison) was built on the orders of William of Orange.

- **Fort Augustus**: This Highland village was called Kiliwhimin (*Cille Chuimein*) until General Wade built a fort there in 1715 and named it after the Duke of Cumberland.

- **Fort George** was built north of Inverness after the '45 Rising. It has room for 2,000 soldiers and is named after King George II.

GLOSSARY

bannock: flat, round bread

bonnet: soft hat

byre: barn

canna: cannot

Catholic: form of Christianity led by the Pope in Rome

cattle drover: bought cows from Highland farms and took them south to market

cavalry: soldiers on horseback

clansman: member of a Highland clan

couped: fell over

croft: small patch of rented farmland

didnae: did not

dirk: small dagger

feart: afraid

jig: dance

laird: lord, often a clan chief

oatcake: savoury oatmeal biscuit

peat: fertile form of soil used as fuel

plaid: long piece of woollen fabric, often tartan

Protestant: later form of Christianity that didn't want to be led by the Pope

scrugged: pulled down

sea kelp: large brown seaweed

standard: big flag with a royal or clan coat of arms

targe: traditional round Highland shield made of wood and covered in leather

Gaelic pronunciation

camanachd (CA-mun-uch-k)

Loch Nan Uamh (Loch nan OO-uv)

O ba bà mo leanabh (Oh ba baa mo LEH-nuv)

Acknowledgements

History is fascinating, and there are often different opinions about what actually happened because of the way events were reported at the time. I wanted to make sure I heard both sides of the story and tried to dig out the truth, as far as I could, about life in 1745 and the Jacobite Risings. I would like to thank all the people who helped me when I was writing and researching this book. I particularly want to thank author Maggie Craig for being so generous with her time and expertise. Thanks also to Professor Murray Pittock of Glasgow University, and to Callum Black and all the lovely people at the Highland Folk Museum in Newtonmore, for answering my many questions. Any errors that crept in are mine, not theirs. Thanks to everyone at Floris Books for making writing this book such an enjoyable experience.

Paintings and Artists

p.14 **Bonnie Prince Charlie** – Allan Ramsey, c. 1745
p.28 **Viscount Dundee** – John Alexander, 1732
p.30 **Queen Anne** – Charles Jervas, 1736, *after* Godfrey Kneller, 1705
p.35 **James Edward Stuart** – Antonio David, c. 1720
p.35 **King George I** – studio of Godfrey Kneller, 1714
p.42 **Rob Roy Macgregor** – W.H. Worthington, c.1820s
p.43 **King George II** – John Shackleton, c. 1755–67
p.57 **General Cope** – artist unknown, 1745
p.87 **Lady Anne Mackintosh** – artist unknown, c. 1745–46
p.89 **Duke of Cumberland** – Joshua Reynolds, c. 1759
p.121 **Flora MacDonald** – Richard Wilson, 1747
p.123 **Charles Edward Stuart** – Hugh Douglas Hamilton, c. 1785
p.123 **Clementina Walkinshaw** – artist unknown, c. 1740–45

Linda Strachan is an award-winning author of over 70 books. An inspirational speaker in schools, libraries and at conferences, Linda is also a Patron of Reading and former Chair of the Society of Authors in Scotland.

Darren Gate is an illustrator and graphic designer based in Scotland. He won the Kelpies Design & Illustration Prize in 2016. He currently lives in Glasgow with his partner and 3 loud budgies.